PENGUIN PROBLEMS

BY JORY JOHN ILLUSTRATED BY LANE SMITH

RANDOM HOUSE 🏠 NEW YORK

To Alyssa and my mom, Deborah
—J.J.

To Sylvie
—L.S.

Text copyright © 2016 by Jory John
Jacket art and interior illustrations copyright © 2016 by Lane Smith
All rights reserved. Published in the United States by Random House
Children's Books, a division of Penguin Random House LLC, New York.
Random House and the colophon are registered trademarks of
Penguin Random House LLC.
Visit us on the Web! randomhousekids.com
Educators and librarians, for a variety of teaching tools, visit us at
RHTeachersLibrarians.com
Library of Congress Cataloging-in-Publication Data is available upon request.
ISBN 978-0-553-51337-0 (trade) — ISBN 978-0-375-97465-6 (lib. bdg.) —
ISBN 978-0-553-51338-7 (ebook)
MANUFACTURED IN CHINA
10 9 8 7 6 5 4 3 2 1
First Edition

Book design by Molly Leach

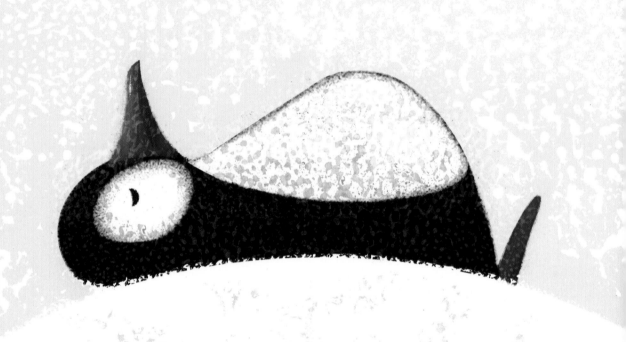

It's way too early.

My beak is cold.

What's with all the squawking, you guys?

It snowed some more last night,
and I don't even like the snow.

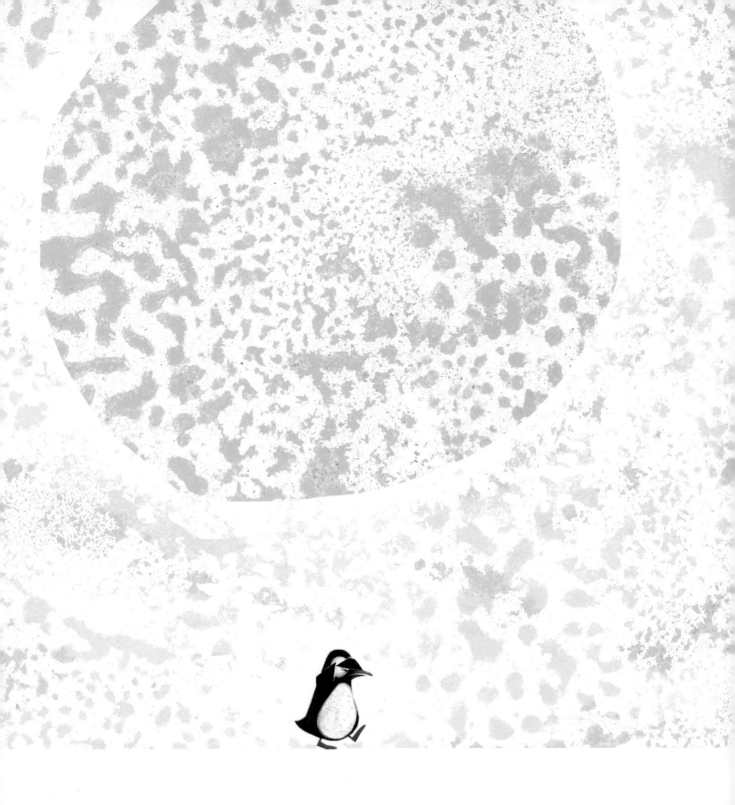

It's too bright out here.

I'm hungry.

I'd like a fish.

Where are all the fish?!

HEY!

FISH!

GET OUT HERE!

The ocean smells too salty today.

I'm not buoyant enough.
I sink like a dumb rock.

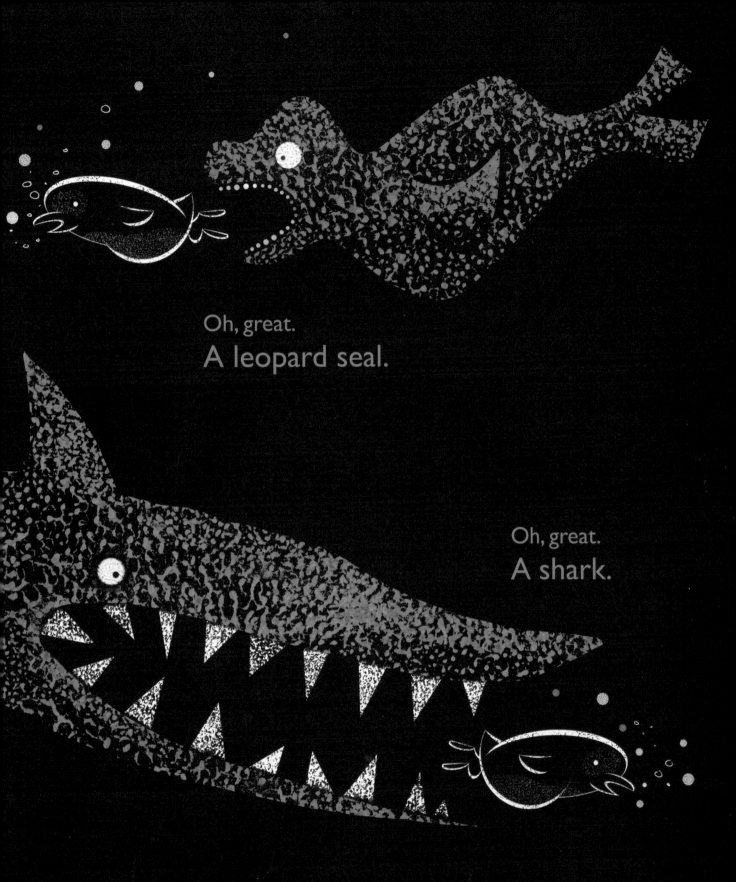

I don't like being hunted.

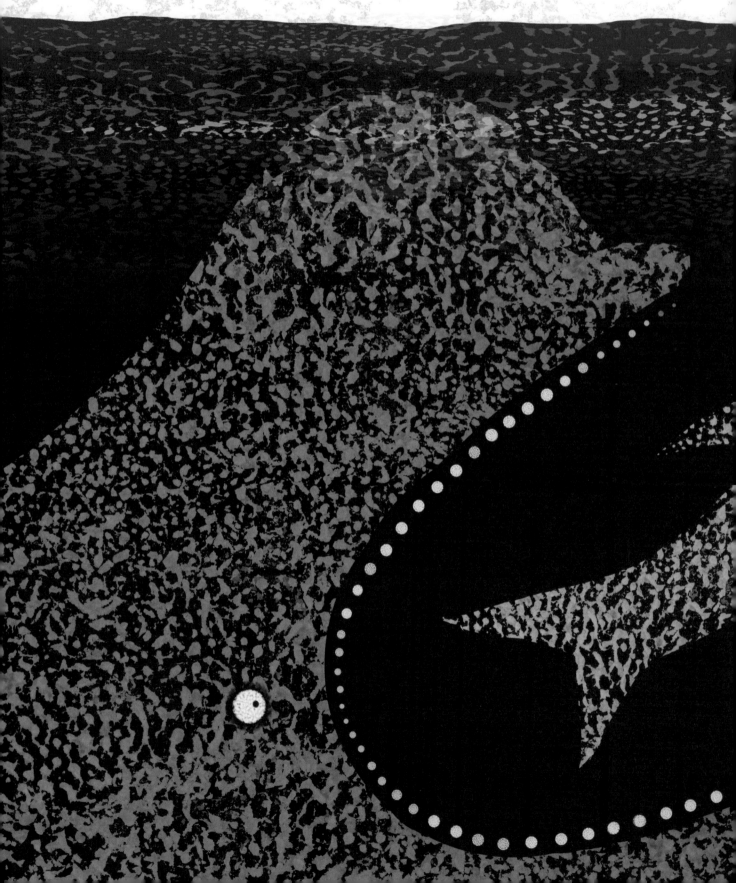

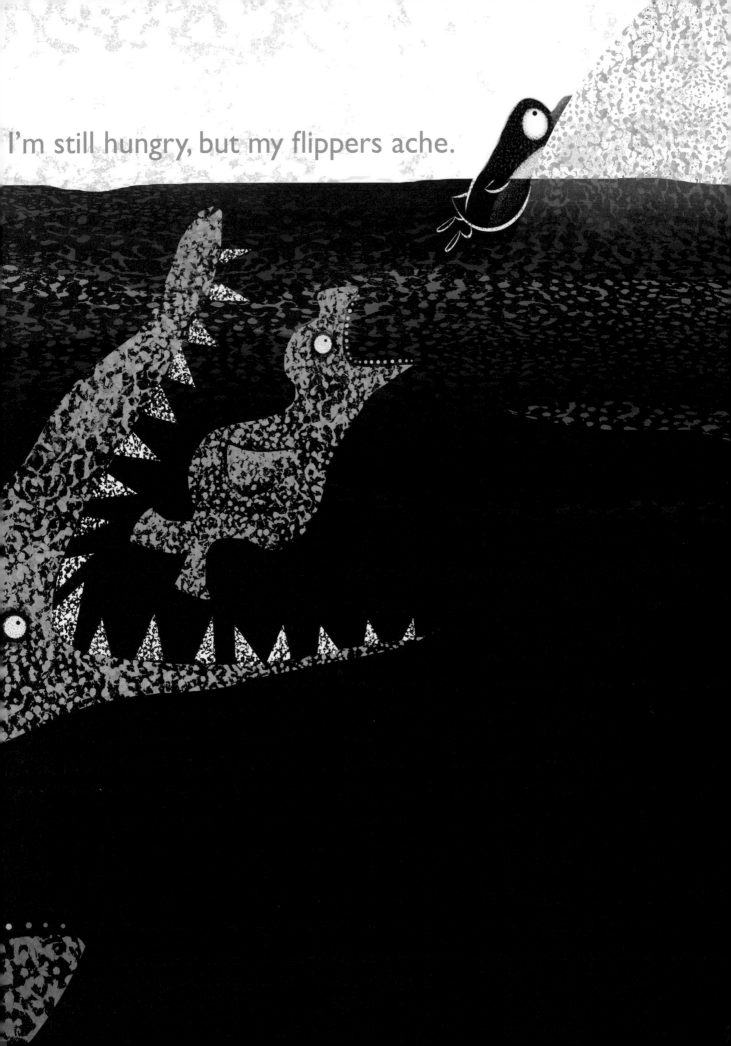

I'm still hungry, but my flippers ache.

I waddle too much. I look silly when I waddle.

See?

I wish I could fly, but I can't.

See?

Everybody looks the same as me.

I look the same as everybody else.

Dad?

I literally have no idea what you're talking about.

My name is Mortimer.

I have so many problems!

And nobody even cares!

I sense that today has been difficult, but lo! Look around you, Penguin. Have you noticed the way the mountains are reflected in the ocean like a painting? Have you gazed upon the blue of that cloudless, winter sky, my friend? Have you felt the sun as it gently warms your back? Have you simply stood with your penguin brothers and sisters and elders, who adore you?

Yes, some things are challenging out here. Yes, we all have difficult moments, from the walruses to the polar bears, from the whales to the penguins. But hear me now, my new friend: I wouldn't trade my life for any other, and I am quite sure you wouldn't, either. I am certain that when you think about it, you'll realize that you are exactly where you need to be.

Please think about what I've said, Penguin.

Goodbye for now.

Who the heck *was* that guy?!
Why do strangers always talk to me?
Walruses don't understand *penguin problems*!

Sigh.
OK, OK.

Maybe that walrus has a point.
After all, I *do* love the mountains.

And the ocean.

And the sky.
And I have friends and family.
This is my only home, and this is my only life.
Maybe things will work out, after all.

My beak is cold.

It gets dark way too early.